This book belongs to:

....

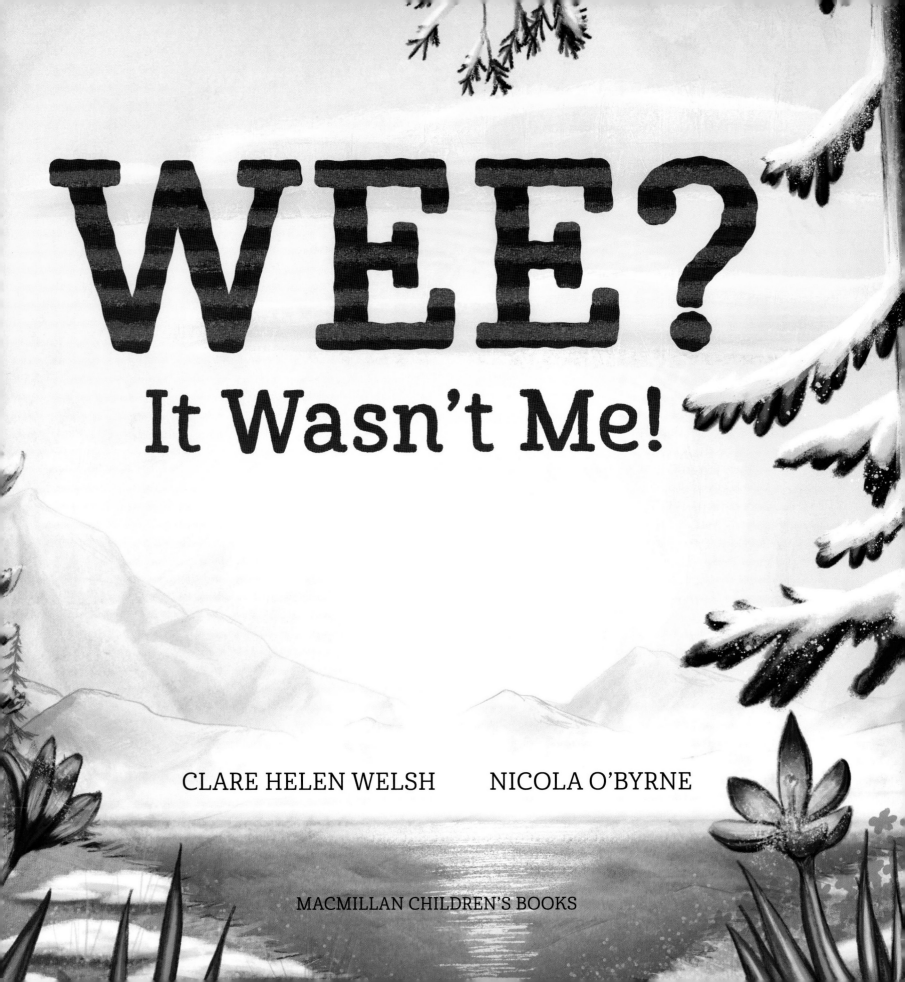

WEE?
It Wasn't Me!

CLARE HELEN WELSH   NICOLA O'BYRNE

MACMILLAN CHILDREN'S BOOKS

Lenny the Lemur was on holiday in Alaska. He was skipping across the snow in the spring sunshine, when he slipped in a puddle. It was wet and yellow and SMELLY!

"Yuck!" said Lenny. "Is that . . .

. . . wee?!"

"It wasn't me!" said
the grey wolf, prowling
over the frozen ground.

"I do my wees on trees. Like this."

"Hmmm," thought Lenny. The wolf's wee didn't look
or smell like the **puddle of piddle** he had slipped in.
"But if it wasn't you, then who?" said Lenny. **"Whose wee
could it be?"** Lenny was determined to find out, so off he set.

"Wee? It wasn't me!" said the leatherback turtle, swimming in the shallows. "I wee through my mouth and then rinse, like this."

Swish! Swash!

"Sound's tasty . . ." said Lenny, stifling a giggle. "But if you didn't **piddle** the **puddle**, then who did? Wee doesn't just fall out of the sky!"

"Oops, sorry!" called the bald eagle, nesting in the trees above. "That was me! But the other one wasn't. I poop and wee at the same time. It's squishy and white."

"Yuck!" huffed Lenny, mopping a **splatter** of **splodge** from his brow. "But if it wasn't you, then who? **Whose wee could it be?**"

Suddenly the wind picked up. A stuffy, musky, bitter smell wafted under Lenny's nose and a mountain goat wandered into view.

"Wee? It wasn't me!" said the goat. "I spray myself in mine. It helps me make friends. Want to see?"

"Thanks, but no thanks!"
said Lenny, holding his nose.

Anyway, he didn't care
whose **puddle** of **piddle** it
wasn't. He only wanted to know
whose **puddle** of **piddle** it was!

Lenny was no closer to finding the culprit and more fed up than ever, when he came across a beaver gnawing wood.

"Was it you? Was it yours?! Are you responsible for that **piddle puddle**?!" he puffed.

"How rude!" glared the beaver. "I haven't even been today! Well, not yet." And with that, out shot a fountain of sweet and sticky **piddle** at Lenny's feet.

"Brilliant!" said Lenny. "This day just keeps getting better and better."

Poor Lenny was miserable.
The **puddle** of **piddle** must have
come from someone.

But if it wasn't the grey wolf, the leatherback turtle,
the bald eagle, the mountain goat or the beaver . . .
then who? **Whose wee could it be?**

Lenny was about to
give up altogether, when
along came . . .

. . . a caribou. "You! It was you, wasn't it?!" Lenny said.
"You peed the **puddle** of **piddle** I slipped in!"

The caribou turned to Lenny and poked out his long tongue.
"I knew it! It isn't funny! My fur is covered in wee!"

But the caribou wasn't making fun. He lowered
his tongue to the ground to take a slurp.

"WAIT! STOP!" Lenny yelled.
"That's not water. It's . . . !"

Too late.

"...WEE!"

"I know..." smiled the caribou,
licking his lips.

"Wee is nutritious and delicious
and this one is full of salts.
I travel miles just to drink it."

Lenny felt a little bit sick.
The other animals did, too.

Except the goat, who
thought it might be
worth a try.

But as the caribou turned to leave, Lenny had an idea.

"Wait! You know all about wee!
If you didn't **piddle** that **puddle**,
then who did?" he asked.

The caribou gave the yellow **puddle** of **piddle** a closer look.

Then he gave
it a sniff.
SNIFF! SNIFF!

And another lick,
just to be sure.

"I've got it," he said. "Follow me!"

Lenny couldn't wait to find that stinky, smelly **puddle-piddler** and tell them off. He and the other animals followed the caribou over, under, through . . .

. . . until, finally, they arrived at the entrance to a cave.
A very BIG cave.

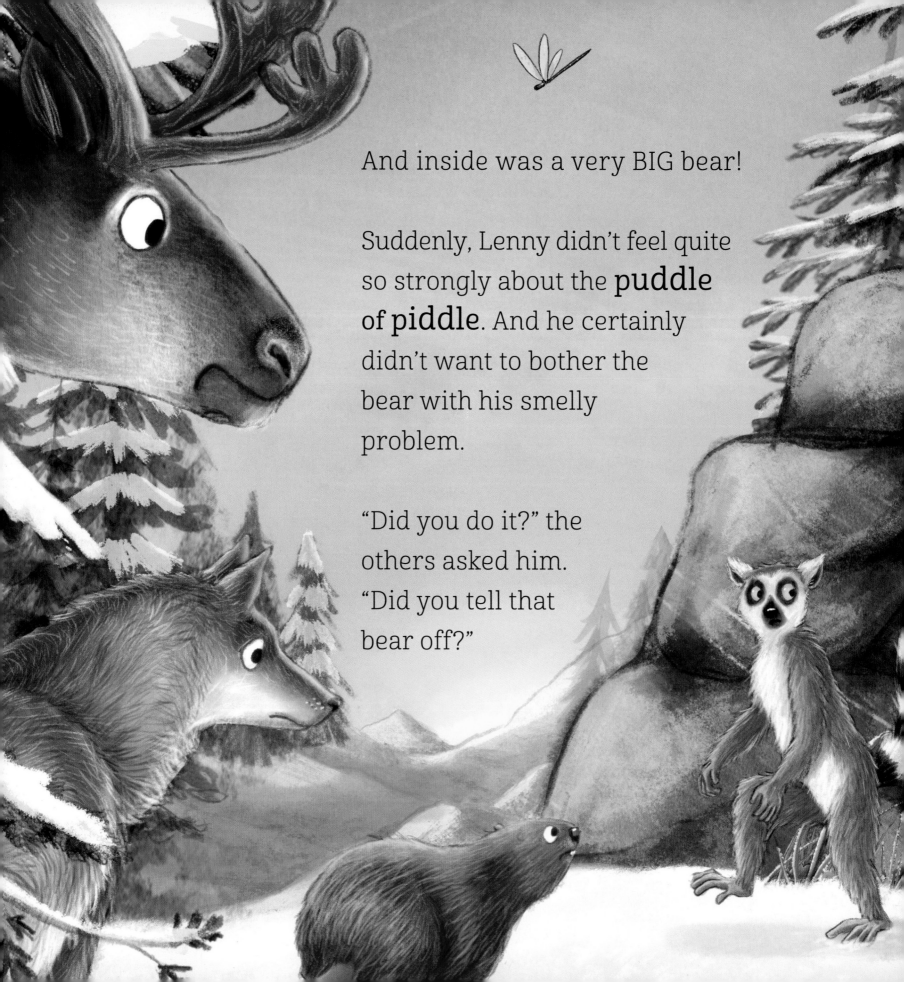

And inside was a very BIG bear!

Suddenly, Lenny didn't feel quite
so strongly about the **puddle
of piddle**. And he certainly
didn't want to bother the
bear with his smelly
problem.

"Did you do it?" the
others asked him.
"Did you tell that
bear off?"

"Er . . . not exactly . . ." said Lenny.
"She was sleeping . . ."

. . . so I left a
message!"

FACTS AND SNAPS!

Male **Grey Wolves** lift up their legs to wee. This lets them aim it nice and high – just at nose level. Perfect for marking territory!

Leatherback Turtles swish water around, then spit it out to get rid of waste. Kind of like weeing through your mouth . . . Tasty.

Like all birds, **Bald Eagles** poo and wee at the same time. But don't worry if bird poop lands on you, as it's said to be lucky.

To attract females, **Mountain Goats** spray themselves with wee, on their faces, beards, chests and front legs. Lucky ladies!

Beavers produce a scent-marking goo, which makes their wee smell like vanilla. Some people even cook with it. Beaver goo biscuit, anyone?

Wee is full of minerals and salts – the perfect snack for wandering **Caribou**. They're particularly fond of human wee.

If you ever go camping in Alaska, don't wee too close to your tent. **Brown Bears** can smell wee from up to five miles away. Watch out, Lenny!

For Finnley, Summer-May and Chloe – C.W.

For Linds and Elena x – N.O'B.

First published 2021 by Macmillan Children's Books
an imprint of Pan Macmillan
The Smithson, 6 Briset Street, London, EC1M 5NR
Associated companies throughout the world
www.panmacmillan.com

ISBN: 978-1-5290-3049-5 (PB)
ISBN: 978-1-5290-5215-2 (EB)

9 8 7 6 5 4 3 2 1

A CIP catalogue record for this book is available from the British Library.

Printed in China.